I WAS SO SILLY!

Big Kids Remember Being Little

collected and illustrated by **Marci Curtis**

 DIAL BOOKS FOR YOUNG READERS   NEW YORK

DO YOU LOVE HEARING STORIES ABOUT YOURSELF WHEN YOU WERE LITTLE?

Do you flip through photo albums laughing at how cute (or goofy or weird!) you were? Are you the star of your favorite home movie?

This book got started after I had interviewed my daughters' friends for a school newspaper project. The kids told me so many funny, crazy, interesting things, I laughed myself silly! Being a mom, a writer, a photographer, and a former kid myself, I started wondering if maybe I could write a book with their help.

I visited three schools near me and sat in teeny-tiny chairs talking to hundreds of kids about their memories of being little. Now they know me as that nosy lady who asks them to speak S-L-O-W-L-Y and repeats everything they say back to them just like a parrot. Even though some kids told me they'd *never* been a baby(!), I still ended up collecting more memories than my book could hold.

Taking the pictures was fun. At one point a boy was having trouble pretending to fling applesauce at me. Finally, I suggested he *really* do it. A gleam appeared in his eye and suddenly his aim improved. I was still picking applesauce out of my ear the next day!

I'm so thankful for all the kids who let me capture a moment of their childhood so I could share it in this book. When my own mother first saw the photos I had taken, she asked me where I'd found such beautiful children. Well, these kids aren't models and they weren't paid. They're totally real kids—just like you. Take a look at what they've shared.

Can you find reminders of the smart, amazing, *and* silly little kid you used to be—and maybe still are?

For my parents, Judy and Bill Watson—thanks for filling my childhood with such great "rememberies," and for supporting the me I used to be.

And a multitude of thanks to the staff, teachers, and parents at Michele's Montessori, Steps Montessori School, and Chestnut Hill Elementary School.

And a special thank you to all 300 children who participated, as well as those who appear uncredited in the book: Alec, Alexis, Hope, John, Josh, Maija, Nicholas, Peter, Rohan, Shannon, Taylor, Vincon, Warren, and all the faceless moms and dads!

Published by Dial Books for Young Readers • A division of Penguin Putnam Inc. • 345 Hudson Street • New York, New York 10014 • Copyright © 2002 by Marci Curtis • All rights reserved • The title is the creation of Dial Books for Young Readers • Designed by Kimi Weart • Text set in Futura • Printed in Hong Kong on acid-free paper • 10 9 8 7 6 5 4 3 2 1 • I was so silly!: big kids remember being little / collected and illustrated by Marci Curtis. • p. cm. • Summary: Records the thoughts of over fifty children between the ages of two and six on such topics as being born, the best part about being little, and growing up. • ISBN 0-8037-2691-0 • 1. Children—Miscellanea—Juvenile literature. 2. Infants—Miscellanea—Juvenile literature. • [1. Children—Miscellanea. 2. Babies—Miscellanea. 3. Children—Quotations.] I. Curtis, Marci. • HQ781 .M35 2002 305.23—dc21 2001037108

The illustrations were created using color negatives that were computer scanned
and then de-saturated with selected portions either re-saturated or colored.

Being Born

I liked to stay in my mommy's stomach. It's messy in there. I hung on to her bones. Then I'd see my two grumpy sisters **yelling** at me, so I wanted to stay in there.

Jessica, 4

God made me. Did you know God made hisself too? He made the whole **world** and that's gotta be hard.

Joshua, age 5

I camed out of my mom's tummy. I remember it well. It feeled like *ticklish*. Then I growed up.

Cameron, age 5

Tales from the Crib

To Do List:
1. End world hunger
2. Negotiate world peace
3. Cure Cancer
4. Develop Alternative Energy
5. Research Preschools.

**Once upon a time
I was such
a smart baby!**

Grace, age 4

I was **wild**—the king of the wild—when I was a baby.

Carson, age 5

I bended my legs over to my head and bited my toes.

Ben, age 4

When I was a baby, I sucked on paper and trees and tables and giraffes. I was a pretty sucky kid.

Nathan, age 3

I liked saying "Goo goo ga ga." It's the baby language, you know.

Piyush, age 4

You know, when I was born, I did a lot of good stuff like eating all my applesauce, but mainly I was just naughty.

Ethan, age 4

When I was a baby, I wore teeny-tiny, eeny-weeny diapers. Now I wear little underpantsies.

Taylor, age 5

When I was one, I teached myself to stand up, and then I could walk. When I was a baby, I thought I'd have to crawl myself to kindergarten.

Benjamin, age 5

When I was one, I ate dog food.

Cassidee, age 6

The last time I was a baby, I didn't have a dog, not a turtle, not a ghost, not a cat. Just an ant . I have all those things now.

James, age 5

Me? I wasn't a baby. I was four, but I was this big. I was never a baby, just a **big boy**.

Josh, age 4

It Was the Best of Times . . .

The best part was jumping on the beds!

Benton, age 5

Getting my face all dirty with spaghetti sauce. **Sometimes I still just dip my face in it.**

Shea, age 6

I liked playing in the mud. **I still do.**

Sydney, age 5

I liked to play makeup with **lipstick** and all sorts of makeup. Lots and lots of makeup.

Madelaine, age 2

I liked that you don't have to do **anything** for yourself.

Annie, age 5

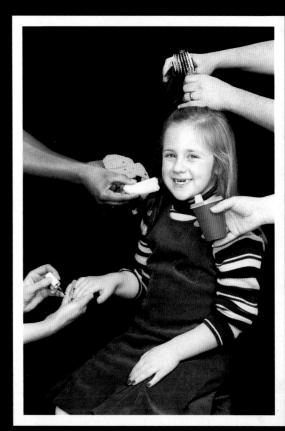

I liked to play with my mom. We played *tackle*.

Gabby, age 5

My favorite part was going to sleep—but I never get to sleep anymore. I miss sleeping.

Zackery, age 5

I liked that I was an only child for a while. I had Mommy and Daddy to myself all the time.

Skye, age 6

It Was the Worst of Times

**I didn't like to be a baby.
All the time people feeded
me oatmeal for no reason.
Oatmeals is nasty.**

DaJervon, age 4

Ghos-tes under my bed. I said, "Hey, I might have to look under my bed to see if there's any ghos-tes." But they're invisible, so I never see anything. It's very frustrating.

Harrison, age 5

I didn't have to dress myself. I don't like having to do it myself.

Amber, age 5

The worse thing is nightmares. Once I dreamed a nightmare about my brother being an alien. He had an alien head, a human body, and a diaper on.

Steven, age 6

I hate fighting with babies. Mom always makes them win.

David, age 5

Stuff I Used to Get Away With

I liked flushing paper down the toilet at home. That's what I did when I was a baby.

Nathan, age 3

I **cut** off all my braids—two up here and two back here. When I looked in the mirror, I thought I looked okay.

Vanessa, age 6

When I was little, I made a *mess* of the whole house. You're not gonna tell my mom, are you?

Grace, age 4

I used to put underwear on my head.

Brian, age 4

Whenever my mom asked me to do something, I'd shake my head and yell: "NO, NO, NO!" I used to say "NO!" to everything.

Elizabeth, age 6

One time I pulled my brother's hair. He just smiled. He didn't mind 'cause I was a baby and he's my brother.

Abby, age 5

One time I put all kinds of (Band-Aids) all over me.

Alyssa, age 6

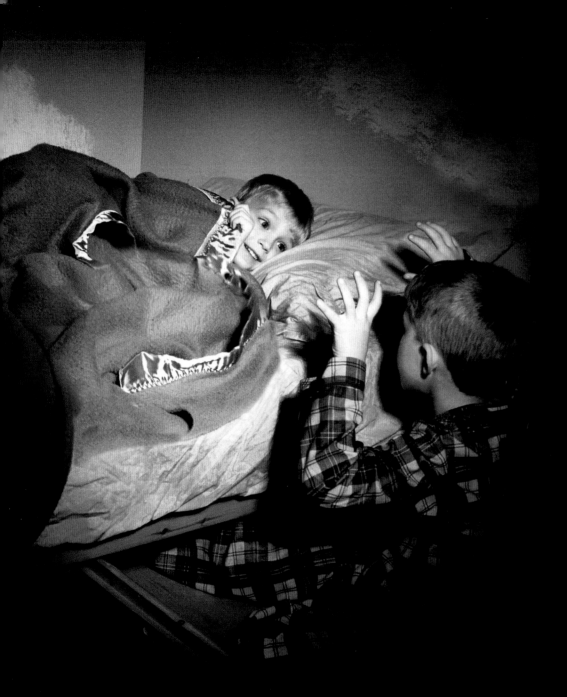

Scary Stories

When I was a little baby there was something scary in my drawer. It was just my brother.
Andrew, age 3

Bears scared me when they  at me. Now I'm a big girl—six and a half—and they're scared of me!

Maddie, really only age 4

I was scared of one of my friends' mom. Then my friend was afraid of my mom. Everything seemed so silly when we were both scared of moms.

Meri, age 5

My dad used to be a werewolf and that scared me, but I guess I'm just used to all that stuff now.

Taylor, age 5

Some of my favorite books used to scare me.

Megan, age 5

I used to be afraid of the dark, but I have a little light I turn on when I get a little afraid, and then the dark disappears.

Alexandria, age 4

Nothing scared me when I was a little child, NOTHING!

Grace, age 4

Things I Miss Most

I miss when my hair
sticked up.
Cassandra, age 5

I wish that I could still be able to wear babies' clothes, because they looked so cute on me.

Mackenzie, age 4

I miss Grandma when I growed up. Grandma died.

Benjamin, age 5

I got to cry.

Keyle, age 6

I miss my fish. I had two  fish and poof! There goes one. So we got another and poof! It died too! We gived up on them.

Brady, age 5

I miss swinging in the baby swing. Even when I was five, I used to, but maybe I'm too big.

Zachary, age 6

I can't put food on my head anymore.

Gabe, age 4

I wish I was still a **baby** because then everybody would still call me cute.

Billy, age 4

I miss that my mom can't carry me.
Kobina, age 5

The Me I'm Going to Be

I was *cute* when I was a little girl—and I still am!

Kalie, age 6 that day

I have this blanket that I always *drag* around with me. My mom wants to get rid of it, but I love it. Pretty soon I'll have to get rid of that thing.

Katie, age 5

I'm very proud and happy that I'm going to be growing up.

Kayla, age 3

If I get bigger,
I'll turn into a
giant.
**I WANT TO STAY
LITTLE FOREVER!**
Meghan, age 3